Sam Can't Sleep
Somos8 Series

© Text: Davide Cali, 2020
© Illustrations: Anna Aparicio Català, 2020
© Edition: NubeOcho, 2021
www.nubeocho.com · hello@nubeocho.com

Text editing: Rima Noureddine, Rebecca Packard

First Edition: April 2021
ISBN: 978-84-18133-06-0
Legal Deposit: M-17024-2020

Printed in Portugal.

SAM
CAN'T SLEEP

Davide Cali   Anna Aparicio Català

nubeOCHO

It's the middle of the night, and Sam can't sleep.

Restless and curious, Sam wants to know why he can't sleep.

"Good evening, Elephant. It is very dark and I can't sleep. Do you know why?"

"I wish I knew... Now please go away. It is very late and I want to sleep."

"Hi, Snake. I have a problem.
I can't sleep. Do you know why?"

"I don't, dear. Can you ask someone
else and let me sleep?"

Monkey? Monkey, are you awake?

"I am now, thanks to you!"

"I can't sleep. Would you be so kind as to tell me why?"

"Would you be so kind as to go away?"

"Hi, Tiger. Sorry to bother you, but do you know why I can't sleep?"

"No, and I don't really care. And if you don't leave immediatly, I'm going to eat you!"

"Gazelle, sorry to wake you.
Can I ask you a question?"

"No, you can't. My baby is sleeping,
so please go away!"

Sam is about to give up when he
sees Crocodile.

"I don't know why everyone is in such
a bad mood tonight. I can't sleep and
nobody cares," Sam says.

"Are you surprised you can't sleep?"
Crocodile asks.

"Shouldn't I be?"

they sleep during the day! Now, how about you fly away and let everyone else sleep?"

As the sun rises,
Sam finally falls asleep...

But now, the jungle is awake...

Hissing and roaring! Bellowing and shouting! Trumpeting and croaking!

"HEEEEEEY!"

Sam shouts.

"Can you please keep it down?
Someone is trying to sleep here."